Soupy
Saturdays

with
the
Pain
&
the
Great
One

OTHER BOOKS BY JUDY BLUME

Picture and Story Books

The Pain and the Great One
The One in the Middle Is the Green Kangaroo
Freckle Juice

The Fudge Books

Tales of a Fourth Grade Nothing
Otherwise Known as Sheila the Great
Superfudge
Fudge-a-Mania
Double Fudge

For Middle-Grade Readers

Iggie's House
Blubber
Starring Sally J. Freedman as Herself
It's Not the End of the World
Are You There God? It's Me, Margaret.
Then Again, Maybe I Won't
Deenie
Just as Long as We're Together
Here's to You, Rachel Robinson

For Young Adults

Tiger Eyes
Forever . . .
Letters to Judy

Judy Blume

Soupy Saturdays

with the Pain & the Great One

ILLUSTRATIONS BY James Stevenson

Delacorte Press

Published by Delacorte Press
an imprint of Random House Children's Books
a division of Random House, Inc.
New York

www.randomhouse.com/kids

Educators and librarians, for a variety of teaching tools, visit us at
www.randomhouse.com/teachers

Library of Congress Cataloging-in-Publication Data
Blume, Judy.
Soupy Saturdays with the Pain and the Great One / Judy Blume ;
illustrated by James Stevenson.
p. cm.
Summary: Revisits the sometimes challenging relationship between a
six-year-old (The Pain) and his eight-year-old sister (The Great One).
ISBN 978-0-385-73305-2 (trade) — ISBN 978-0-385-90324-0 (GLB)
[1. Brothers and sisters—Fiction. 2. Sibling rivalry—Fiction.] I. Title.
PZ7.B6265Sou 2007
[E]—dc19   2006026892

The text of this book is set in 15-point Goudy.

Printed in the United States of America

10 9 8 7 6 5 4 3 2 1

First Edition

For Eli and Hannah Block,
who are never a pain,
and almost always great!
—J.B.

For Edwina
—J.S.

CONTENTS

The Pain

Meet
the
Pain

My sister's name is Abigail. I call her the Great One because she thinks she's so great. She says, "I don't think it, I know it!" When she says that I laugh like crazy. Then she gets mad. It's fun to make her mad. Who cares if she's in third grade and I'm just in first? That doesn't make her faster. Or stronger. Or even smarter. I don't get why Mom and Dad act like she's so special. Sometimes I think they love her more than me.

The Great One

Meet
the
Great One

My brother's name is Jacob but everyone calls him Jake. Everyone but me. I call him the Pain because that's what he is. He's a first-grade pain. And he will always be a pain—even if he lives to be a hundred. Even then, I'll be two years older than him. I'll still know more about everything. And I'll always know exactly what he's thinking. That's just the way it is. I don't get why Mom and Dad act like he's so special. Sometimes I think they love him more than me.

3

Mr. Soupy

On Saturdays we do errands with Dad. He's good at errands. Today, even though it was really warm, the Pain was wearing earmuffs. Big fluffy ones. Our first stop was the shoe store. The shoe salesman took one look at the Pain and said, "We have some nice snow boots on sale. Half price."

"Why would I want snow boots in May?" the Pain asked.

The shoe man shrugged. "Looks like you're getting ready for winter," he said, pointing to the Pain's earmuffs.

"I'm getting ready for a haircut," the Pain told him.

"Oh," the shoe salesman said, as if that made perfect sense.

The Pain got a pair of sandals. So did I.

From the shoe store the three of us walked up the street to Mr. Soupy's. Mr. Soupy is our haircutter. You have to be under twelve to have Mr. Soupy cut your hair. In the window of his shop there's a sign. It says

Mr. Soupy sings while he snips your hair. "No more than an inch," I reminded him when it was my turn.

"A big inch or a little inch?" Mr. Soupy sang.

"A little inch," I said.

I knew when Mr. Soupy was done because he whipped off my cape and shook out the hair. I watched as it floated to the floor. It looked like more than an inch to me.

Then it was the Pain's turn. But he was

still outside. He looked over at Dad. Dad was in the waiting area, reading a magazine. Then the Pain looked at me.

"What?" I said, even though I knew *what*. The Pain is scared of haircuts. He didn't used to be scared. Nobody knows why he's suddenly weird about them. Maybe he knows. But if he does, he's not telling.

Finally, he climbed up into the chair.

"Hmmm . . ." Mr. Soupy said, walking around him. "It's hard to give a good haircut when a person is wearing earmuffs."

The Pain just sat in the chair pretending he couldn't hear a word. I lifted one of his earmuffs halfway off and talked right into his ear. "Mr. Soupy says he can't give you a good haircut while you're wearing earmuffs."

As soon as I said it I started wondering if Mr. Soupy is his real name. Probably not. It's probably just some name he invented. If it *is* his real name I wonder if it's his first name or last? Probably his last. I wonder what his first name is? Sam Soupy? Scott Soupy? *Zachariah* Soupy?

Mr. Soupy tried to get the Pain to take off his earmuffs. He made silly faces. He did a wild dance. But he wasn't getting anywhere. The Pain just sat there.

Finally, I said, "Why don't you try it with just one ear covered? That way, if Mr. Soupy doesn't cut off your first ear you'll know you're safe."

The Pain didn't answer.

"Look around," I told him. "Do you see anyone without two ears?"

The Pain looked at the kids who were waiting.

They looked back at him.

"That doesn't mean it *can't* happen," he said. "Besides, if Mr. Soupy cut off *your* ear would you come back?"

"The only cut you get at my shop is a *haircut!*" Mr. Soupy sang. Then he laughed at his own joke.

I laughed with him.

But the Pain didn't even smile.

"You can cut the back," the Pain told Mr. Soupy. "You can cut the front. But you *can't* cut around my ears. Those are the rules."

"Okay," Mr. Soupy said. "No problem."

"You can do that?" the Pain asked.

"Sure."

"Won't he look funny?" I said.

"Sure," Mr. Soupy said. "But he didn't say he cared about looking funny."

Mr. Soupy raised his scissors to the Pain's head. As soon as he did, the Pain let out a wail. . . . *"Waaahhhh!!!"*

11

That got Dad's attention. He came over to the chair. "What's up?" Dad asked.

Mr. Soupy put down his scissors and said, "I give up!"

"You can't give up," Dad said. "You're Mr. Soupy. You get the job done!"

Mr. Soupy sighed. "Bring him back in a few days," he told Dad. "When I don't have a crowd waiting."

At home, the Pain said, "I'll grow my hair long and wear it in a ponytail."

"Okay," Mom said. "Fine."

"Fine?" I asked her. "How can you say that's fine?"

"What's the problem?" she said. "If Jake wants a ponytail, he can grow a ponytail."

"George Washington had long hair," the Pain said. He was racing two little cars around Mom's chair. Fluzzy was trying to catch them.

Oh, excellent! I thought. *My brother's going to look like George Washington.* "Are you going to get wooden teeth, too?" I asked him. "Because George Washington had wooden teeth. Did you know that?"

The Pain opened his mouth and showed off *his* teeth.

Three weeks went by. The Pain's hair was flopping in his eyes.

"How long does it take to grow a pony-tail?" he asked.

"A long time," I told him.

"How long?" he asked.

"All summer, at least."

"All summer?" he repeated, as if he couldn't believe it.

I offered him barrettes. He knocked them out of my hand. Fluzzy batted them around on the floor. I tried not to laugh.

The next day I said, "I have an idea." I got some cardboard, a pair of scissors, my best markers, and some string. Then I made the Pain a set of cardboard ears.

"Green ears with pink dots?" the Pain said when I was finished.

"Why not?" I asked, attaching them to his ears.

"Suppose Mr. Soupy cuts through the cardboard?" the Pain asked.

"He won't."

"How do you know?"

"Did you ever try to cut through cardboard?" I said.

The Pain checked himself in the mirror. "I look like someone from another planet."

"You act like someone from another planet," I told him.

"That's how much you know!" he said.

But the next Saturday, he wore his green ears with the pink dots to Mr. Soupy's shop.

"Nice ears," Mr. Soupy said.

"Thanks," I said. "I made them."

"Good job," Mr. Soupy said.

I had to agree.

Mr. Soupy got to work. He saved the ear trim for last. The Pain closed his eyes. I whispered, "I didn't want to tell you until now, but these ears have magical powers."

"What powers?" the Pain asked. He opened his eyes and looked at me.

I whispered, "If Mr. Soupy gets too close to an ear . . ."

"What?" the Pain said. "What will happen?"

"Mr. Soupy will find out," I said.

"Stop!" Mr. Soupy said. "You're scaring me."

But I noticed how carefully he trimmed around the Pain's ears.

When Mr. Soupy was done, he whipped the cape off the Pain. The hair fell to the floor. The Pain looked down at it. "Can I have some of that hair?" he asked.

"Help yourself," Mr. Soupy said. "No extra charge."

The Pain jumped out of the chair. He scooped his hair off the floor and mashed it into a ball.

Mr. Soupy handed him a little bag.

"What are you going to do with all that hair?" I asked.

The Pain shrugged. "You never know." Then he put his green ears back on.

"You are *so* weird," I told him.

"I know," he said. "That's why you're glad I'm your brother."

"Who says I'm glad you're my brother?" I asked. "Did I ever *say* I'm glad you're my brother?"

"No, but you made me ears," the Pain said.

"So?"

"So you must like me."

"Like you?" I said, as if that was the craziest thing I'd ever heard.

"If you didn't like me, why would you help me?" he asked.

"Help you?" I said, as if that was the second-craziest thing I'd ever heard. "I wasn't trying to help *you*! I was trying to help Mr. Soupy get the job done!"

The Pain

Soccer Doc

On Saturdays I'm going to play in a soccer league. Just like the Great One. And here's the best news—Justin's dad is the coach!

We have a uniform. It's red and blue. It has a jersey, long socks, shin guards, and cleats. I tried it on in my room. Then I raced around the house with my soccer ball, pretending I knew all the moves.

"Watch where you're going!" the Great

One shouted as I tripped over her LEGO village.

"Can't," I told her. "Wherever the ball goes, I go too."

Fluzzy took a flying leap onto the sofa.

"Mommm . . ." the Great One yelled.

"Jake!" Mom called. "Take your soccer ball and play outside."

So I kicked my ball to the front door, then down the steps, across the grass, and back again. *Wait until Justin's dad sees me in action*, I thought.

The next day we had our first practice. Justin's dad said we should call him Soccer Doc because his last name is hard to say. But I know how to say it because it's Justin's last name too. *So Si O Ski.*

I raised my hand and called out, "Dr. Sosioski—what if we know how to say your name?"

"Everybody's going to call me Soccer Doc," he said.

"Even me?" I asked.

"Even you, Jake."

"Even me?" Justin asked, laughing and rolling around on the grass.

Justin's dad took off his glasses. He wiped them on his shirt. Then he took a deep breath and said, "Yes, Justin. Even you."

Justin didn't say anything else. But he sat up and stopped laughing.

Soccer Doc gave us some moves to practice. Dribbling around cones. Passing on lines. Kicking to shoot. One time he blew his whistle and shouted, "Justin . . . pay atten-tion!" But Justin just stood there watching a squirrel col-lecting nuts. Soccer Doc shook his head.

At our first game Soccer Doc made me goalie. When I put on the goalie jersey and the goalie gloves, I felt like a superhero. I could hardly wait for the game to begin.

"You know what your job is, Jake?" Soccer Doc asked. He didn't wait for me to answer. "Your job is to block the ball from going into the net."

"I know that," I told him.

"Good," he said. "I'm counting on you."

The game began. For a long time everybody was at the other end of the field. It's boring being goalie when everyone else is so far away. What was I supposed to do?

Then I saw a dog break away from someone in the stands. The dog ran onto the field. His leash dragged behind him.

"Mookie . . ." a woman called. "Mookie . . . come back here!"

I tried to catch Mookie. But Mookie was faster than me.

Suddenly, both teams started running in my direction. In the stands people were shouting. *Uh-oh!* I ran back to my position. Mookie followed me, barking. While I was trying to shoo him away from the goal, somebody from the other team kicked the ball and—*wham!* He scored a goal. The other team cheered.

Then it was two goals.

Then three.

Four.

Five.

I couldn't stop the ball from going into the net no matter how hard I tried. I wanted to lie down on the ground and cry. But I knew I couldn't.

At dinner the Great One asked about our first game.

"I played goalie," I told her. Then I took a long drink of milk. "I hate being goalie."

"How come?" the Great One asked.

"Because," I said.

"Because why?" she asked.

"Just because." I didn't have to tell her anything if I didn't want to. Besides, I was busy hiding my peas in my mashed potatoes. Why would Mom put peas on my plate when she knows I only eat white food?

"Sometimes I play goalie," the Great One said. "Nobody can score when *I'm* goalie!"

"That's why I don't like being goalie," I said.

"What was the score?" the Great One asked.

"Six–two," I told her.

"Don't feel bad," she said. "It's not *all* your fault." She tried to hide a smile.

"Who says I feel bad?" I asked.

Then Dad said, "It's not about winning or losing. It's about having fun playing the game."

And Mom said, "In the next game you'll be more experi-enced."

But we lost the next game 7–1.

I don't get why the Great One thinks playing on a team is fun. "Do you have fun even when you lose?" I asked her.

"Yes," she said.

"How come?"

"Because *playing* is fun! And Miranda is the *best* coach. She makes us feel good no matter how we play." Then she said, "What's Justin's father like?"

"He's *not* fun," I told her. I ran to my room. I wasn't going to tell her anything else. I wasn't going to tell her how Soccer Doc is always cleaning his glasses. And shaking his head. And how sometimes he says "Nice try"—but you can tell he doesn't mean it.

That night I had a dream. I dreamed I had stomach pains. In my dream I went to Soccer Doc's office. "I have pains in my stomach," I told him.

Soccer Doc poked my stomach. "There's nothing wrong with you," he said. "Go home."

So I went home. But I didn't get better. The next day I went back to Soccer Doc's office. I said, *Nice try, Dr. Sosioski!* I said *Nice try* the way he does at soccer. I said it so he could tell I didn't really mean it.

When I woke up my stomach hurt for real. Mom gave me a spoonful of pink stuff and an extra hug. She said, "Grandma is coming to your next game."

We lost *that* game 5–2.

Grandma said, "Soccer looks like hard work to me. All that running around . . ."

"Running is the fun part," I told her. "That's why I don't want to play goalie."

"But you're a good goalie," Grandma said.

"No, I'm not. Half the time I let them score a goal."

"Yes," Grandma said. "But the other half you stop them."

I never thought of that.

The next day, Justin called. "You want to come over?"

"Okay."

"Bring your soccer ball," Justin said.

We played soccer all afternoon. William came by and asked if he could play.

We said, "Sure."

Then Michael came over.

Then Annie and Jenny, who are in fourth grade.

We had a great time.

Later, Justin walked me home. "I'll tell you a secret if you promise not to tell," he said.

"I promise."

"I like soccer but I don't like soccer league."

"Same," I said.

Then we were both quiet. We sat on the front steps of my house. Finally, Justin said, "I wish I could play goalie."

I was surprised. "You want to play goalie?"

Justin nodded.

"I wish I could play any *other* position," I told him.

"Really?" Justin looked surprised.

Then we just sat there, drawing in the dirt with sticks.

The Great One came out of the house and looked at us. "What's wrong?" she asked.

"Who says anything's wrong?" I said.

"I can tell," she said. "I can read your mind."

Before I could tell her she'll never be able to read my mind, Justin blurted it out. "I want to play goalie and Jake wants to play any position *but*."

The Great One said, "No problem. Tell your coach. You'd think he'd *want* someone else to play goalie since you've lost every game."

"But the coach is his father," I said.

"So?" the Great One looked at Justin. "Just tell him it's not fair that your friend gets to hog the best position."

"*Just tell him?*" Justin asked.

"Duh . . ." the Great One said. "How is he supposed to know if you don't tell him?"

Justin looked at me. I looked back at him.

At our next game I gave Justin the goalie jersey and the goalie gloves.

"What's going on?" Soccer Doc asked when he saw Justin.

Justin said, "It's not fair that only Jake gets to play goalie."

Then everybody else on our team chanted, "We want to play goalie too!"

Soccer Doc shook his head. He took off his glasses. He wiped them on his shirt. Then he took a deep breath and said, "All right. We'll take turns playing goalie."

"And all the other positions too?" I asked.

Soccer Doc looked right at me. I could

feel my heart beating. Finally, he said, "Why not? We'll take turns playing everything."

The team cheered.

Soccer Doc was surprised. He smiled for the first time.

We still lost the game 4–3 but we had fun playing. I even scored a goal. My first. And Justin was a good goalie. Except when he stopped to watch a bird, or a squirrel, or the clouds go by.

The Pain

The Great Pretender

The Great One can't ride a bike. She doesn't want anyone to know. Especially her friends. "What person in third grade doesn't already know how to ride?" I asked her.

She said, "I could ride if I wanted to. But I can go faster on Rollerblades—or a scooter—or a skateboard."

"You don't have a skateboard," I reminded her.

She has a bike. It's blue. It sits in the garage, waiting for her to learn to ride it. "There's no hurry," Mom said last week. "Abigail will learn when she's ready." Mom's been saying that for more than a year. Still nothing.

Sometimes I catch the Great One looking at it. One time I caught her touching it. "It's so easy," I told her. "You just get on and pedal."

"Don't you think I know that?" she said. "If I felt like it I could hop on and ride better than you!"

I laughed because I know that's not true.

I'm not supposed to tell the Great One's friends she can't ride a bike.

"Some things are private," Mom said.

"Some things stay in the family," Dad said.

The Great One said, "If you *ever* tell my friends I can't ride a bike I will *never* speak to you again!"

"Is that a promise?" I asked.

She threw Bruno at me. "And I'll tell all your friends you still sleep with a stuffed elephant!"

"So?" I said. "Dylan sleeps with fifty stuffed animals."

"But does he chew on their ears?" she asked.

"I don't chew on Bruno's ear!" I shouted.

"Then how come it's wet and slobbery in the morning?" she asked.

I didn't answer. I'm never going to tell her about Bruno's ear.

On Saturday I was riding my bike in front of our house. The Great One was blading behind me. "Ha, ha! Abigail can't ride a bike!" I sang as I flew by her. "Abigail can't ride a biiiike!"

"Shut up, you little twig!" she yelled.

"Twig?" I called, zooming around her. "What's a twig?"

"A stick!" she yelled. "And that's what you are. You're a little stick! I could break you in half if I wanted to."

"You'd have to catch me first," I called, racing up the street.

Later, the Great One's friends rode their bikes over. Emily called, "Hi, Abigail—we're riding to Sasha's house. Want to come?"

"Sure," the Great One said. "But my bike is being fixed."

"Still?" Kaylee asked.

"Yes," the Great One said. "They can't figure out what's wrong with it. So I'll go on my blades instead."

Emily said, "It will take you forever on your blades."

"No, it won't," the Great One told her. "I'm a whiz on my blades. Bet I'll get to Sasha's house before you."

"Okay," Kaylee said. "Let's race." And

her friends took off on their bikes.

As soon as they were gone, the Great One ran into the house and asked Mom for a ride to Sasha's house. She said, "I have to get there before my friends. It's a race and I told them I'd win on my blades."

"Abigail . . ." Mom said.

"Please, Mom . . . just this one time," the Great One begged.

"Abigail . . ." Mom said again.

"Pretty, pretty please with strawberries on top?"

"Abigail," Mom said. "This is getting out of hand."

"This is the last time," the Great One said. "I promise."

Mom looked at the Great One.

The Great One whispered, "I can't tell my friends."

"I'll bet they'd understand," Mom said.

"Please don't make me tell them."

Mom sighed. Then she grabbed her car keys.

The Great One got into the car wearing her blades. I jumped in too. "Let me off a block away," the Great One said to Mom.

Mom stopped the car before we got to Sasha's house. The Great One jumped out and bladed away.

As we were driving home I asked Mom, "How come it's okay for the Great One to lie to her friends?"

"It's not exactly lying," Mom said. "It's more like pretending."

"Pretending she can ride a bike?" I asked.

"Pretending she can blade faster than they can ride," Mom said.

"It sounds like lying to me," I told Mom.

"Sometimes it's not that easy to tell the difference," Mom said. "And sometimes you have to let people figure things out on their own."

But I *have* figured it out on my own. And I say the Great One is lying!

That night I told her so. "Liar, liar, liar!" I sang while I jumped on her bed.

"Get off my bed, *stick*!" she yelled. "Get out of my room or you'll be very, very sorry!"

I could tell she meant it, so I took off. The second I was gone she slammed her bedroom door.

Later, when she thought I was asleep, I heard her on the phone. "Hello, Emily," she said. "I have something to tell you. . . ."

I got out of bed and tiptoed over to my door. Fluzzy followed me. I put my ear right up against the door so I wouldn't miss anything.

"You know my bike?" I heard the Great One say. "Yes, the one that needs to be fixed . . .

Well, here's the thing. . . ."

That's when I sneezed. A big, noisy sneeze. I couldn't help it. It just came out. Fluzzy jumped. The Great One shrieked. Then she said, "Emily . . . I'll call you right back. As soon as I . . ." Then she mumbled something I didn't get. Something that ended with ". . . *my brother.*" I knew it wasn't good. I ran back to bed, pulled up my blanket, and pretended I was asleep. Fluzzy jumped on top of me.

Two seconds later my door opened. "Jacob Edward Porter!" the Great One shouted. *Uh-oh! She used my whole name.* "Were you spying on me? Because if you were, you are in Big Trouble . . . capital B, capital *T*!"

The Great One marched over to my bed. "I know you're not really asleep. People don't sneeze while they're sleeping." She poked me. "Wake up!"

"*What?*" I sat up and acted really surprised. I held Bruno against me.

"You can't fool me!" she said. "You were spying."

"I was sleeping. You woke me up."

"Ha!" she said. "I know exactly what you were doing. I *always* know exactly what you're doing."

"No, you don't," I said. "You don't know anything."

"No more spying or I'll tell."

"Spying is better than lying," I shouted as she marched away.

She stopped. She turned. She looked right at me. "So you admit you were spying?"

"If you admit you were lying," I said.

"I'm not a liar!" she said. "I'm a great pretender. And I *can* ride a bike. I just don't like to fall."

"Is that what you were going to tell Emily?"

"That proves it! You *were* spying. And if I ever catch you spying again, you will be *sorrier* than sorry." She walked out, shutting my bedroom door behind her.

This time I didn't bother to get out of bed when I heard her say "Hello, Emily . . . it's me again." This time I didn't have to spy. I already knew what she was going to say. Fluzzy and I just laughed to ourselves. Then we fell asleep.

The Great One

Party Girl

I'm having a sleepover party on Saturday night. I've been waiting all my life to have one and now it's finally happening. Emily, Sasha, and Kaylee are coming to celebrate my half birthday.

My real birthday is on July fourth. Every year our family has a picnic. All the aunts, uncles, and cousins come. Every year it's the same. Oh, sure—they sing "Happy Birthday" to me. But the cupcakes have red, white, and blue sprinkles on top.

On Saturday night everything will be different. On Saturday night everything will be pink. *Pink, pink, pink!* It's going to be the best party ever. It could be the best party in the history of the world. And one of the reasons is, the Pain won't be here. He won't be here to toot his horn, or jump on my bed, or sing stupid songs at the top of his lungs. He won't be here because he's going to Grandma's house.

He cried when Mom told him. "This proves it," he said. "You love Abigail better than me!"

"Sweetie," Mom said to him. "I know this is disappointing, but there will be other birthday parties."

The Pain looked at me. I reminded him that he doesn't eat chocolate. And the frosting on my cake is going to be gooey, yummy double chocolate.

"What about the roses on top?" he asked.

"Pink," I told him. "Pink roses with green leaves."

"Oh," he said. "I thought they would be white."

I could tell he was disappointed. I tried not to feel sorry for him. I mean, why should I feel sorry for him? It's not my fault he only eats white food. It's not my fault he doesn't know how to behave around my friends.

By the end of the week all I could think about was my party. *Saturday, Saturday, Saturday*, I sang inside my head. My teacher, Mr. Gee, said, "Abigail . . . are you with us? Abigail, are you listening?"

"What?" I asked.

"Where are you, Abigail?" Mr. Gee said.

"I'm here," I told him.

"I'm glad to hear that," Mr. Gee said. "Then maybe you can answer my question."

"I don't know the answer," I said. I didn't know the question, either, but I didn't tell that to Mr. Gee.

Madison Purdy laughed. I don't like Madison Purdy.

On Friday night I couldn't fall asleep. I got out of bed and tiptoed down the hall looking for Fluzzy. I found him in his usual place. On the Pain's bed. I don't understand why Fluzzy likes to sleep on the Pain's bed when he could sleep on mine. It's so unfair—especially since I'm the one who feeds him. I lifted Fluzzy off the bed, careful not to wake the Pain. I carried him into my room and put him down on my bed. He opened his eyes and yawned. "Go back to sleep, Fluzzy," I told him.

But Fluzzy started licking his paws. He made that slurpy sound he makes when he's grooming. It's impossible to sleep while Fluzzy is grooming. So I carried him back to

the Pain's bed. Fluzzy gave me one of his looks. I know what he was thinking. *Why can't Abigail make up her mind?* Then I ran back to my bed and dove under the covers.

Finally, I must have fallen asleep, because when I opened my eyes it was morning. I ran to my window. It was a gray, sleety winter day. I opened my window wide and stuck out my head. *Brrr*—it was freezing. But so what? For once, my party would be an inside party.

I ran through the house, checking to see who was awake.

Not the Pain.

Not Fluzzy.

And not Mom or Dad, either.

Maybe they forgot about my party, I thought. I stood over them until Mom opened her eyes. She made room for me under her quilt. I snuggled next to her. She was warm and she smelled sleepy.

"Today's your big day," she said, quietly, so she wouldn't wake Dad.

"I thought you forgot," I said.

"How could I forget such an important event?" she asked.

That's when Dad opened his eyes. He said, "What event?"

"My half birthday party," I told him.

"Oh, that's right," Dad said. "Do I have to wear pink too?"

I laughed. "No, Dad. I don't think pink is your color."

Then the Pain came into the room and flopped on the bed. "My throat hurts. So does my head."

"He's just saying that!" I told Mom and Dad. "He's just saying that because he wants to stay home and ruin my party." As soon as I said it I felt bad because I could see he was really sick. He looked terrible.

"What party?" he whispered. He could hardly talk.

"My half birthday party," I told him.

"Oh, that . . ." he said, as if he didn't even care.

Dad felt his forehead. "He's hot," he said to Mom.

"Uh-oh," Mom said.

Dad took him to Dr. Bender's office. When they came back the Pain lay on the living room sofa. He said, "I have to take medicine. I might throw up."

"I'd better call the other mothers," Mom said.

"What other mothers?" I asked.

"Your friends' mothers. I have to tell them Jake is sick."

"No . . . don't tell them," I begged. "Please don't tell them. Let him go to Grandma's house."

"I can't send him to Grandma's house now," Mom said. "That wouldn't be fair to Grandma or Jake."

"What about me?" I asked. "It's not fair to me, either. This proves you love him better than me."

"Honey," Mom said, "I know this is disappointing, but . . ."

I felt tears stinging my eyes. I wanted

to go to my room, shut the door, lie on my bed, and cry.

Mom said, "Let's see what the other mothers say."

I already knew what Sasha's mom would say. And I was right. She told Mom Sasha couldn't come because Sasha gets asthma from every little cold.

Kaylee's mom said Kaylee had been up all night, sick. She had a fever of a hundred and three, just like the Pain.

My party was falling apart.

But Emily's mom said she could come. She said they don't worry about germs in their family because they've got four kids and someone is always sick in winter. "Isn't that good news?" Mom asked when she was off the phone.

"A party with just one friend?" I said.

"One friend is better than none," Mom said.

When I called Emily she said, "Do I still have to wear pink?"

"Yes," I told her. "It's still a Princess in Pink party."

"I hate pink," she said.

But when she came to my party she was wearing a pink shirt. "I borrowed it from my sister," she said. Then she handed me a present wrapped in pink paper. "Happy half birthday. It's from Sasha and Kaylee, too."

"Thank you," I said. I opened the box. Inside was a pink book with blank pages and a sparkly pink pen. "I love it," I told her. "It's perfect."

"Good," she said. "I hate to give presents that no one likes."

Then we sat at the table to make our princess tiaras. Each one came with a bag of jewels. You got to stick on the diamonds, rubies, and emeralds yourself.

Emily said, "These aren't real jewels, are they?"

"No," I told her. "Real jewels would cost zillions."

"I thought so," Emily said.

We wore our tiaras while we ate our pizza.

We wore them while we watched my favorite princess movie.

When the movie ended, Emily said, "I've never wanted to be a princess. I want to be a vet when I grow up. Or maybe an explorer."

"You think I want to be a princess?" I asked.

"Don't you?" she said.

"No—it's just a party thing," I explained.

"Oh," she said. "I'm glad to hear that."

Now I'll never be able to tell her the truth. I'll never be able to tell her that actually, I wouldn't mind being a princess.

After the movie, Mom lit the candles on my cake. She and Dad and Emily sang "Happy Half Birthday" to me. That's when the Pain came downstairs and into the kitchen. He was

carrying Fluzzy over his shoulder.

"Jake," Mom said, "you're supposed to be in bed."

"Fluzzy smelled ice cream," the Pain said.

59

"That's impossible," I told him. "A cat can't smell ice cream from so far away. And neither can a human—especially a *sick* human." I looked at Mom. "Make him go back to his room."

"Ice cream would help Fluzzy's sore throat," the Pain said.

"Since when does Fluzzy have a sore throat?" I asked.

"He caught it from me."

"Would Fluzzy like a scoop of vanilla?" Mom asked the Pain.

"If it's the white vanilla," he said. "Fluzzy doesn't like the yellow vanilla."

Emily looked at me. "What's he talking about? Vanilla is vanilla."

I didn't even try to explain.

Dad said, "I'll keep Jake company upstairs while Fluzzy has his ice cream."

After we finished our cake and ice cream, Emily and I went up to my room. She looked at the two sleeping bags laid out side by side on the floor. Then she looked at me. Then

she looked back at the sleeping bags. Then she said, "I think I'll go home now."

"But it's a sleepover party," I reminded her. "You can't go home. You'll ruin everything if you go home now."

"I'm sorry," Emily said, "but I want to go home."

"Is it because of my brother?"

"Your brother?" Emily said. "It has nothing to do with your brother."

"Then what?" I asked, choking up.

"I just want to go home," Emily said. She sounded choked up too.

I found Mom and told her Emily wanted to go home.

Mom asked Emily if she was feeling okay.

"Yes," Emily said. "But I want to go home."

"Are you sure?" Mom said.

Now Emily got teary for real. "Yes, I'm sure."

Mom called Emily's house. Her dad

explained that Emily has never slept over at *anyone's* house. He said, "This was going to be her first time. But I guess she's not ready yet."

"Don't be mad," Emily said to me at the door. "It was a good party. I liked the cake. Can I take my tiara with me?"

I nodded.

My sleepover party, the one I'd waited for all my life, was over. And it wasn't even nine o'clock. Mom put her arm around me. "This was the worst half birthday party in the history of the world," I told her. I tried not to cry but it wasn't easy.

"I'm sorry it didn't turn out the way you'd hoped," Mom said. "Maybe next year . . ."

But I didn't want to think about next year.

The next morning the Pain came into the kitchen. "I need juice."

Dad poured him a glass. He asked the Pain if he was feeling better.

"A little," the Pain said. He eyed the two

extra tiaras on the counter. "Can I have one of those?" he said.

"You want to be a princess?" I asked.

"No, I just want a crown," he told me.

"Help yourself," I said. "I'm *so* over everything princess!"

He took a tiara and a bag of fake jewels. He stuck the jewels on the tiara. Then he put it on his head—backwards. He looked so silly I started to laugh.

"Next year you better have a white cake for your half birthday," he said. "Because I'm coming to your party."

"Don't worry," I said. "I'm not having any more half birthday parties. This was my first and last."

"What about your regular birthday?"

"What about it?"

"I'm coming to your party, right?"

"You always do."

"And you can come to mine," he said. Then he ran to the hall mirror to look at himself in his tiara.

While he was gone I cut myself a huge slice of birthday cake. It tasted even better than last night.

The Pain

Olive One

Aunt Diana is going on a trip. "Maybe she'll bring the baby to stay with us," the Great One said. "And I'll be the babysitter." She started lining up baby toys. Some of them were mine.

"The baby doesn't like you," I told the Great One.

"Does so!" the Great One shouted.

"Does not!" I shouted back. I picked up my old horn and tooted it at her.

She covered her ears and called, "Mommmm!"

I laughed. I love to make the Great One mad.

Mom came out of the kitchen. She was making soup. She always makes soup on Saturday mornings. She said, "Children . . . the baby will like both of you when he's older."

"But he'll like me better," the Great One said. "Because I know how to babysit."

"No, you don't," I told her.

"Yes, I do!" The Great One put her hands on her hips. She glared at me. I laughed again.

"You are such a pain!" she shouted.

"Children," Mom said again. "This is a silly argument." Then she went back to the kitchen.

"Silly, silly, silly!" I sang, dancing around the Great One and all the baby toys.

The Great One tried to kick me. But I'm faster and jumped out of the way. Fluzzy sniffed an old windup monkey. "Stop that!"

the Great One told him. "That's for the baby, not you."

When the doorbell rang the Great One called, "I'll get it!" But she ran so fast she tripped over the hall rug and fell flat on her face. I felt like laughing but I didn't. Instead, I opened the door.

It was Aunt Diana holding the baby. "Ooooh," the Great One called, picking herself up off the floor. "I knew you'd bring the baby."

The baby's name is Jackson. But everyone calls him *the baby*. I wonder if they'll still call him *the baby* when he starts school. I feel sorry for him if they do.

Aunt Diana shoved the baby at the Great One. "Abigail, would you hold him for a minute?"

"I *knew* you'd want me to babysit," the Great One said.

As soon as the Great One took the baby, the baby started to cry. The Great One patted him on the back. "You're going to like me soooo much," she cooed.

The baby cried louder.

"I'm going to be your favorite babysitter," she sang. "You'll see."

Aunt Diana wriggled off her red backpack.

Now the baby was screaming.

"Maybe he's tired," Aunt Diana said, reaching for the baby. She stuck a pacifier in his mouth. The baby stopped crying.

"Where's your mom?" Aunt Diana asked. She looked at her watch. "I don't want to miss my plane."

"Here I am," Mom said, coming from the kitchen. She wiped her hands on her jeans. "I was just getting ready for Olive."

"I don't like olives," the Great One said. She wrinkled her nose. "You *know* I don't like olives."

Neither do I, but I didn't say so. I never agree with the Great One if I can help it.

Aunt Diana laughed. "You're a picky eater, Abigail. I hope the baby won't be a picky eater."

"I'm *not* a picky eater," the Great One said. "I just don't like olives. You want to see a picky eater, look at Jake. He only eats white food."

"Yeah, but I'm not picky," I told her. "I'll eat *any* white food."

"No, you won't," the Great One said. "You won't eat cauliflower."

"Cauliflower has green stems."

"That's enough," Mom told us. "Aunt Diana is in a hurry."

Aunt Diana handed Mom the red backpack. "Everything you'll need is right in here," she said. "Food, vitamins, toys, treats, brush, special blanket, and a list of emergency numbers just in case."

"Don't worry," the Great One said. "I'm going to be the best babysitter in the history of the world."

"Olive will be glad to know that," Aunt Diana told her.

"Olive?" the Great One said. "Who's Olive?"

I was wondering the same thing.

Aunt Diana opened the front door and whistled. A scruffy old dog walked up to the house. "This is Olive," Aunt Diana said. "She's staying with you while I'm away."

"A dog?" the Great One cried, as if she

couldn't believe it. "A dog! I thought you were leaving the baby."

Aunt Diana smiled. "Not this time."

The Great One looked at Olive. Olive looked at the Great One. Then the dog barked. Fluzzy practically flew up the stairs.

"Maybe Olive will think you're the best doggy-sitter in the history of the world," I said.

"Shut up!" the Great One shouted.

But I was already rolling around on the floor and Olive was licking me.

The Pain

Olive Two

Fluzzy doesn't like Olive. He's been hiding in the closet since Olive got here. We think he comes out to eat in the middle of the night. Poor Fluzzy. Maybe he doesn't like the way Olive smells.

"Dog breath," my friend Justin said. "We should brush her teeth."

So we tried. I put plenty of toothpaste on

my toothbrush. But Olive wouldn't open her mouth.

"We need a treat," I told Justin. So we went to the kitchen. Olive followed us. I knew she would. She loves to eat.

I got out a treat and showed it to Olive. She opened her mouth, and when she did, Justin got the toothbrush inside. But Olive bit down on it and Justin couldn't get it out of her mouth.

"That's *my* toothbrush!" I said.

"*Was* your toothbrush," Justin said.

Finally, Olive dropped the toothbrush. There was no toothpaste left on it.

Olive licked her chops. When she opened her mouth I smelled my toothpaste.

Later, Dylan came over. "That's a smelly dog," he said, holding his nose.

"She's a rescue dog," I told him. "She's old."

"What's a rescue dog?" Dylan asked.

"A dog who needs a home."

"Maybe she needs a bath," Dylan said.

So we filled the bathtub. We threw in some of the Great One's bubble bath.

The bubbles came up so high we were sure they would hit the ceiling.

Olive sniffed them. Some got stuck to her nose. But she wouldn't get into the tub.

She growled when Dylan tried to pick her up. "Is she going to bite me?" he asked.

"No," I told him.

"Are you sure?" Dylan asked.

"Pretty sure. Just don't try to pick her up again."

"Don't worry," Dylan said.

"Maybe a shampoo would work better," I said, looking at Olive.

"Yes, a shampoo," Dylan agreed.

"Come on, girl," I said to Olive. "You're going to like this." I dug another treat out of my pocket and waved it in front of Olive's face. She followed me into Mom and Dad's bathroom. They have a walk-in shower.

I rubbed some shampoo into Olive's fur. It smelled nice, like coconut.

"That's not enough," Dylan said. "Olive is a big dog. She needs a lot of shampoo." He grabbed the bottle and poured it onto Olive's back. I rubbed it in. Olive's fur turned white and sudsy. "She smells better already," Dylan said.

It was true. She did.

I showed Olive another treat and she followed me into the shower. But when I turned
on the water Olive jumped out without

getting wet. I wasn't so lucky. I got soaked.

Dylan laughed his head off.

Suddenly, the bathroom door opened. The Great One stood there with her hands on her hips. "What are you doing?" she shouted. "And what's wrong with Olive?" She ran her hand over Olive's back. "Is this shampoo?" she asked, smelling her hand.

"Yes," I told her.

"Are you out of your mind?" she said.

Before I could answer—before I could say *No, I'm not out of my mind*, she yelled, "You can't use people shampoo on a dog."

"Says who?" I asked.

But the Great One didn't answer. She marched out of the room and yelled,

"Mom . . . Dad . . . we have an emergency!"

Mom and Dad both came running.

"Uh-oh," Dad said. "What's happened to Olive?"

"We were just trying to shampoo her," I explained.

Dylan didn't say anything.

Mom looked at me and said, "Jake, you're all wet. Go and change your clothes."

So I went to my room. I got out of my wet clothes. I pulled on sweatpants and a hoodie. Then I flew down the stairs in time to see Dad hosing off Olive in the yard. The Great One was wearing rain gear even though it was a sunny day. She was trying to hold Olive still.

"You better pray Olive doesn't catch cold and die," the Great One said to me. "How would you explain *that* to Aunt Diana?"

I started to worry.

Dylan said, "Dogs swim even when it's cold out. What do they care about water from a hose?"

But I could see that Olive cared. I felt really bad for her.

"Get some towels, Jake," Dad called. "We have to dry off this dog."

But Olive had other plans. She started shaking the water off her coat. She shook and shook, spraying water everywhere. At Dad, at Mom, at Dylan, and at the Great One. "*Stop it, Olive!*" the Great One shrieked.

But Olive didn't stop until she wanted to.

That night we were playing Monopoly when Fluzzy came out of hiding. He batted around one of Olive's toys. Then he carried it away in his mouth. "Did you see that?" I asked. "Fluzzy just stole one of Olive's toys."

"Borrowed," the Great One said. "Fluzzy doesn't steal."

That's when the phone rang. I answered. It was Aunt Diana. She wanted to know if Olive was having fun.

"Yes, Olive is having a lot of fun," I told Aunt Diana.

"What's she been doing?" Aunt Diana asked.

For a minute I wasn't sure what to say. Then I got an idea. "Today we played dentist," I said.

"Dentist!" Aunt Diana said. "Was Olive the dentist or the patient?"

I got this picture in my mind of Olive trying to brush *my* teeth. "We took turns," I told Aunt Diana.

Then I looked at Olive. She looked back at me with those big brown eyes. And I knew that even if she could speak, she would keep our day a secret from Aunt Diana.

"Thanks, Olive," I said.

Weirdo on Wheels

Olive stayed with us for a week. On Saturday we took her back to Aunt Diana's house. Before we got going Dad stacked our bikes on the car rack. "Don't bother taking mine," I told him. But he took it anyway.

"Are you going to ride your bike today?" the Pain asked.

"None of your business," I told him. "Are you going to get carsick today?"

"None of your business," he said. Then he laughed.

Aunt Diana lives in the country. As soon as we got going, Olive stuck her head out the car window. I like Olive. She's a good dog. There's just one problem. Even after her bath, she's still the smelliest dog in the history of the world. I covered my face with a towel so I wouldn't have to smell her.

It took an hour to get to Aunt Diana's house. For once, the Pain didn't get carsick. And Olive was very glad to see Aunt Diana and Mitchell. Mitchell is Aunt Diana's husband. We don't call him Uncle. We just call him Mitchell. Or Mitch. He's very tall. He's so tall he can reach anything. Aunt Diana doesn't need a step stool since she married Mitch.

At their wedding, the Pain stuffed his pockets with mini hot dogs in tiny rolls. That was before he decided to only eat white food. Mom found the hot dogs the next morning when she was putting away his clothes. The mustard made a mess of his jacket. That's what you get when you take the Pain to a wedding.

Aunt Diana had lunch ready when we got to her house. Soup and sandwiches. The Pain ate white cheese on white bread. When we finished, I helped Aunt Diana clear the table. "Did you enjoy taking care of Olive?" she asked.

"Oh, yes," I told her. "Olive is a very nice dog. There's just one thing. . . ."

"What's that?" Aunt Diana asked.

"It's about Olive's smell," I said.

"What smell?" Aunt Diana asked.

"You know," I said. "The bad smell."

"What bad smell?" Aunt Diana asked. Then she put her face right up close to Olive's and she cooed, "You don't smell bad, do you, girl?"

Olive licked Aunt Diana.

I decided not to say anything else.

Then Mom called, "Who wants to go for a bike ride?"

"I do," Dad answered.

"Me too," the Pain sang. "Come on, Abigail—let's go!"

"No, thank you," I said. "I'm going to stay here and play with the baby."

The Pain gave me a look.

When the three of them were gone, Mitchell said, "Hey, Abigail . . ."

Mitchell hardly ever says anything. When he does, he talks very softly. You have to listen carefully or you'll miss what he's saying. "There's no traffic on our road," he told me. "It's a good place to learn to ride a bike."

I pretended I didn't hear him.

"Abigail . . ." he said, louder. Then he repeated what he'd just said—about how their road is a good place to learn to ride a bike.

"No, thank you," I told him. "I'm playing with the baby."

"Actually," Aunt Diana said, "the baby is ready for his nap." She scooped up Jackson and carried him away.

I could feel Mitchell looking at me. "I'll

just sit here and read," I told him. "I brought a book."

"You know, I'm a pretty good teacher," Mitchell said. "I teach seventh- and eighth-grade math."

"What does math have to do with riding a bike?" I asked.

"Well . . . some kids think they can't learn math," Mitchell said, "so they're afraid to try."

"I'm good at math," I told him. *I'm good at other things too, I thought. I can blade better than anyone I know. I can jump rope, turn an almost-perfect cartwheel, and make pancakes with hardly any help. The Pain is hopeless at those things. So how come he can ride a bike? It's so unfair.*

"All it takes to ride a bike is practice," Mitchell said.

"Practice *falling?*" I said. "No, thank you."

Mitchell opened a bag. He pulled out padded pants and a padded shirt. He pulled out knee pads, elbow pads, wrist guards, padded gloves, and a helmet with a face guard. He stuck the helmet on my head.

"Where'd you get all this stuff?" I asked.

"I collect it," Mitchell said. "Just in case."

"Just in case *what?*" But I was thinking, *Hmm . . . maybe with all this padding I should try. . . .* Then I thought, *No, I have tried. . . .* Then I thought, *Yes, but if I don't try one more time, I'll never know. And this will positively, absolutely be my final try. . . .*

So when Mitchell held out the shirt, I took it and pulled it on. It was way too big. So was everything else. But Mitchell didn't care. Soon I was padded everywhere. I was so padded I waddled like a penguin.

Mitchell led me to the front door. I caught a glimpse of myself in the hall mirror. *No one would recognize me in all this stuff*, I thought. *No one would know it's me, Abigail Carly Porter, from 10 Larken Road.*

"Riding a bike is like learning to swim," Mitchell told me. "Once you learn you'll never forget."

"I'm good at swimming," I said. Then I added, "Not like my brother, who's afraid to put his face in the water."

"You'll be good at bike riding too." I shook my head. Mitchell patted my back. "You'll see," he said.

I reminded him to make sure the seat on my bike was very low. I reminded him that I needed to be able to put my feet on the ground whenever I wanted. Mitchell held the bike steady as I got on. My knees were shaking. My stomach felt funny.

"Now . . . close your eyes," Mitchell said.

"Close my eyes!" I said. "Are you crazy?"

"Come on, Abigail. Just *close* your eyes and *feel* yourself balance on the bike."

"I can't!" I cried. "I can't!"

"Yes, you can," Mitchell said.

"Promise you won't let go?"

"I promise."

So I closed my eyes. *Maybe I'll never open them*, I thought.

"Okay," Mitchell said. "Very good. Now let's give it a try."

His voice was so soft I wasn't sure what he said. So I didn't move. I just sat on the bike with my eyes closed.

"Abigail," Mitchell said. "Open your eyes and pedal."

"Pedal?" I said, as if that was a crazy idea.

"Yes, pedal."

So I started to pedal. I pedaled very, very slowly.

"Faster," Mitchell called. "Pedal faster."

So I did.

"That's it. . . . Keep pedaling."

Mitchell ran, holding on to the back of my bike. As long as he was running with me and holding on to the bike, I was okay. The second he let go, I fell. I was glad I was wearing padded *everything*. "You see!" I told Mitchell. "I knew I would fall."

"You know why you fell?" Mitchell asked. "You fell because you stopped pedaling."

"I always fall when I stop," I told him.

"*Aha!*" Mitchell said.

"Aha, what?"

"*Stop* equals *fall*," Mitchell said. "We've solved the problem."

"What problem?"

"Your problem," Mitchell said, as if he was talking about math. "If you want to stop pedaling, you have to brake and step to the ground. Pedal, brake, step to the ground. Got that?"

"Pedal, brake, step to the ground," I repeated.

"That's it," Mitchell said. "Let's try again."

So I tried again. Mitch held my bike steady until I got going. Then he ran with the bike. I couldn't tell when he let go. I just kept pedaling and pedaling—until I braked—and jumped off my bike. This time I didn't fall. But my bike did. It fell over on its side. Too bad it wasn't padded, like me.

"You know why your bike fell?" Mitch called, running to catch up with me.

I shook my head.

"Because you let go," he said. "When you step off your bike you have to hold on to it."

"You didn't tell me that," I said. "You said 'Pedal, brake, step to the ground.'"

"Well, now you know," Mitch said, very softly. "So, let's give it another try."

"Do I have to?"

"If you want to be able to ride, you do."

I thought about Emily, Sasha, and Kaylee on their bikes. Then I thought about the Pain singing *Abigail can't ride a bike* . . . and how good it would feel to prove he was wrong.

So I tried again.

And again.

And again.

Soon I was pedaling on my own. And instead of running

after me, Mitch was pumping his arm. *Yes!* I reminded myself to hold on to my bike every time I came to a stop. *Pedal, brake, step to the ground. . . . Pedal, brake, step to the ground.* By the time Mom, Dad, and the Pain came back, I was riding up and down the road. I was even practicing wobbly turns. I couldn't wait to tell my friends!

Then I heard the Pain call, "Who's that weirdo on wheels?"

"That's no weirdo," Mitch called back. "That's your sister."

"My sister can't ride a bike," the Pain called.

I whizzed by the Pain, singing, "Oh yes, I can!" Then I tried a show-offy turn, lost my balance, and flew off my bike—right into a big pile of leaves. After a minute I picked myself up. "How about that trick?" I called. "I'll bet you can't do a flying leap like that!"

The Pain shook his head. "This proves it. You *are* a weirdo on wheels!"

"That's why you're glad I'm your sister," I told him.

"Who says I'm glad?"

"Think about it," I said. "You *could* have a boring, ordinary sister. Instead, you have me!"

Then I got back on my bike and rode away, with the Pain calling, "Abigail . . . wait! Abigail . . ." But I was already pedaling as fast as I could. And inside my helmet, I was smiling.

The Last Word from the Great One

The next Saturday it rained. When I went looking for my markers I couldn't find them. "Did you take my best markers?" I asked the Pain.

He said, "Maybe."

So I shouted. "You know you can't take my markers without asking. That's a rule. Give them back. Right now!"

So he threw them at me and laughed.

"Ha ha! Ha ha!"

That really made me mad. So I yelled, "Pick up my markers right now, you little pain. Pick them up and put them back in their box or you'll be very, very sorry."

The Last Word from the Pain

My sister thinks she's so great but this time when she called me a pain I laughed. I laughed and then I said, "And you're such a . . . such a . . ."

And she said, "Such a what?"

And I said, "Such a big bowl of soup!"

And she said, "Everybody likes soup."

And I said, "Not spider soup. And that's what you are. You're a big bowl of spider soup!"

Then she said, "Mmm . . . sounds yummy!"

So I said, "Spider poop soup! That's what you are."

Then she got mad and yelled, "That's it!" And she started chasing me.

I ran as fast as I could, calling, "Mom . . . help! Mommmm! She's after me."

The Last Word from Fluzzy

Oh, good—
They're playing my favorite game.
Run, chase, shout.
You'll be sorry!
I'm telling!
I'm going to get you!

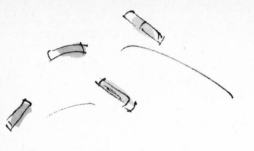

Best is when they throw things.
His elephant.
Her markers.
I run around them so they know I want to
    play too.

The mom and dad don't get it.
They call, *That's enough!*
They call, *No fighting, no biting!*
But fighting and biting are the best parts.
Not scary bites. Just little nibbles.

Oh, listen—
Now they're going to make spider soup.
Spider poop soup.
I've never tasted any kind of spider soup.
I wonder if I'll like it?

I meow, telling them to wait for me.

Judy Blume spent her childhood in Elizabeth, New Jersey, making up stories inside her head. She has spent her adult years in many places, doing the same thing, only now she writes her stories down on paper. Her twenty-five books have won many awards, including the National Book Foundation's Medal for Distinguished Contribution to American Letters.

Judy lives in Key West, Florida, and New York City. You can visit her at www.judyblume.com.

James Stevenson has written and illustrated more than a hundred books for children. In forty years at the *New Yorker*, he has published more than two thousand cartoons and covers, as well as numerous written pieces. His illustrated column "Lost and Found New York" frequently appears on the op-ed page of the *New York Times*.